For Tim

...who sings the fox's song with me.

"...er of the world, it is the only way to survive in it."
— Jansson

Order from www.flyingeyebooks.com

SANDRA DIECKMANN

# The DOG that ate the WORLD

Flying Eye Books

London | New York

Down in the valley, bird sat with bird, bear fished
with bear, and fox played his fiddle to the foxes.

The sound of their play and their laughter
drifted peacefully through the trees...

...until one day, the dog appeared.

He took what he wanted...

...and drank however
much he pleased.

The more he ate, the bigger he became. So the fox stepped forward to play him a song to soothe his terrible hunger.

The dog swallowed him whole! But the fox played on.

His lonely song travelled to the outside

...so three brave bunnies
decided to free the fox.

The dog swallowed them too.

Enough was enough, everyone agreed.
Together they would restore the peace!

But talking to him, tricking and
tiring him out did not change a thing.

The dog swallowed them all!

With nowhere else to go, the animals lit a light.

Together they talked, they worked and hope began to blossom in every heart...

...as life went on.

The greedy dog still ate and ate.

But when he finally swallowed the sun
and the sky, there was nothing left to take.
He had eaten his whole world while...

...theirs was now brighter
and stronger than ever before.

In the end, there was just no place
for someone as greedy as the dog.

Down in the valley, the wind whistled
peacefully through the trees again.

"Wherever we are together, we are at home!"
they all sang while the fox played his song.